No, No Noah!

Dandi Daley Mackall

ILLUSTRATED BY

Elena Kucharik

Tommy NELSON

www.tommynelson.com

A Division of Thomas Nelson, Inc.
www.ThomasNelson.com

Published in Nashville, Tennessee, by Tommy Nelson™,
a division of Thomas Nelson, Inc.

Library of Congress Cataloging-in-Publication Data

Mackall, Dandi Daley.
    No, no, Noah! / Dandi Daley Mackall; illustrated by Elena Kucharik.
      p. cm. – (I'm not afraid)
    Summary: A young monkey is afraid to leave familiar surrounds to
join the other animals on Noah's ark until he decides to trust God.
   ISBN 0-8499-7750-9
   [1. Monkeys—Fiction. 2. Fear—Fiction. 3. Noah (Biblical figure)—
Fiction. 4. Stories in rhyme.] I. Kucharik, Elena ill. II. Title.

PZ8.3.M179 No 2001
[E]—dc21

                    2001042760

Printed in Peru
05 06 07 QW 5 4 3 2 1

"Come down, Monkey!" Noah cried.
"There's the ark! Now run inside!"
But I kept swinging in my tree.
"No, no, Noah! Don't take me!"

"Monkey, Monkey, take my hand!
God intends to flood this land.
Come on down and get in line.
God will see us through just fine."

"Are there trees on your big boat?
Are you sure your ark will float?"

"If I come along with you,
Like those creatures, two by two,
Must I leave all this behind?
No, no, Noah! Never mind."

Sadly, Noah turned away.
"Noah, please!" I hollered. "Stay!
Can't you see it's way too scary?
Is this whole trip necessary?"

"Monkey, you must trust the Lord."
So I prayed and jumped aboard.

Bunking with a kangaroo,
Dining in a floating zoo . . .

Swinging by an alligator.
"Sorry, mister! See you later!"

Neighing,
barking,
cooing,
mooing . . .

Croaking,
    Cockle-doodle-doo-ing!

Forty days it rained and poured.
All the bears and beagles snored.

Then God turned His wet world dry,
Arched His colors in the sky.
Now all day I dance and sing,
With a rainbow for a swing.

When your day brings something new,
Think of Noah's floating zoo.
Pray like Monkey swinging low.
God stays with you as you go!